Becky and Kaia's New Addition

A Tale of Penn State Children's Hospital

Written by Lindsay C. Barry
Illustrated by Susan Szecsi

D1104361

PennState
Health

All rights reserved. No part of this book may be reproduced or transmitted in any form or by any means electronic or mechanical including photocopying recording or any information storage and retrieval system without permission in writing from the Publisher.

Text Copyright © Lindsay C. Barry 2021
Find the Author at lbarrybooks.com

Illustration Copyright © Susan Szecsi 2021
Find the Illustrator at brainmonsters.com

Library of Congress Cataloging-in-Publication Data:
Names: Barry, Lindsay C., author. | Szecsi, Susan, illustrator.
Title: Becky and Kaia's new addition: a tale of Penn State Children's Hospital / written by Lindsay C. Barry; illustrated by Susan Szecsi.

Description: Santa Fe, NM: Santa Fe Writers Project, 2021. | Audience: Ages 5-13. | Audience: Grades 2-3. | Summary: "It's a very special day at Penn State Children's Hospital for Kaia and Becky, the hospital's two facility dogs. This golden dynamic duo has a lot to bark about, including their mission to provide kids and families with emotional support as they navigate their way through their hospital journey"— Provided by publisher.

Identifiers: LCCN 2020040418 (print) | LCCN 2020040419 (ebook) | ISBN 9781951631116 (trade paperback) | ISBN 9781951631123 (ebook)

Subjects: LCSH: Working dogs—Juvenile fiction. |
Penn State Children's Hospital—Juvenile fiction.
Classification: LCC PZ7.1.B37274 Bec 2021 (print) | LCC PZ7.1.B37274 (ebook) | DDC [E]—dc23

LC record available at https://lccn.loc.gov/2020040418
LC ebook record available at https://lccn.loc.gov/2020040419

Published in 2021 by Santa Fe Writers Project
369 Montezuma Ave. #350 Santa Fe, NM 87501
sfwp.com

Printed in the USA

Dedication

Drawing on the expertise of more than 200 pediatric specialists, Penn State Children's Hospital provides nationally recognized, patient-centered health care to kids facing a range of challenges, from complex heart disease to childhood cancers. The hospital is equipped to treat the most severely ill patients, with a highest-level designated neonatal intensive care unit and pediatric trauma center. The number of specialty practices, clinics, and outreach locations continues to grow, which means our kids and families can access extraordinary care close to home.

For the hundreds of thousands of children and families who live in the communities we serve, this means peace of mind and hope for a healthier future.

From building a freestanding, state-of-the-art hospital in 2013 and expanding its footprint in 2020 to funding life-saving equipment, family-centered programs, and transformative pediatric research, our generous supporters prove that we are stronger together.

Our story is only possible because of the incredible teams you support—doctors, nurses, therapists, scientists, and specialists that dedicate their lives to caring for children.

Everyone at Penn State Children's Hospital would like to thank those who were responsible for helping us build an even brighter future for our kids through our new addition. With your help, our journey continues so that we can provide more kids the world's best gift – the chance to write their own story.

We hope you enjoy this tale told through the eyes of our friendly and compassionate facility dogs, Becky and Kaia. Your dedication and support opens up endless pawsibilities for our kids and families. Thank you for helping us write our next chapter.

PennState Health
Children's Hospital

Kaia walked into the bright lobby of Penn State Children's Hospital, ready for the exciting day ahead of her. It was early morning, and the sun streaming through the tall glass windows glinted off her golden fur. Her nails clicked on the shiny floor, and she blinked hello at her blurry reflection in the window.

Kaia heard the swoosh of the electronic doors opening and, with a glance behind her, saw her Child Life partner, Becky, waltz in with her signature sassy tail waggle.

Kaia dropped the tennis ball she was holding in her mouth

and nuzzled Becky, who did the same but kept a grip on her two stuffed toys. Ashley and Erin, their handlers, allowed them to exchange early morning nuzzles and play for a bit before declaring it was time to get to work.

"Okay ladies," Ashley said. "Get ready now – we've got the new addition of Children's Hospital to explore!"

Today was a very important day – they were officially opening the Children's Hospital's vertical expansion, and Kaia and Becky couldn't wait to explore and visit their patients.

Before they could start, the doors swooshed again and a family entered. A little girl with a bright blue cast on her wrist squealed and darted to Kaia and Becky. Wagging their tails, the Golden Retrievers sat still, letting the girl approach them. Even though both dogs sported their special Child Life green vests, the girl was nervous about touching them.

"Don't worry," Erin said. "These dogs are part of the hospital's Child Life team. They help patients feel

comfortable when they need to stay here for a while."
A tiny hand landed on Kaia's head, then Becky's. "I'm Mandi,"
the girl said to the dogs. "I'll be in the hospital for a few days
to fix my wrist so it works better. I got to pick my cast color.
It's blue!" She raised her arm to show them her cast. The
dogs wagged their tails again to show they understood.

"C'mon Mandi, time to go!" Mandi's
mom called. After giving the dogs two
huge squeezes, Mandi said goodbye
and joined her family to check in.

Kaia and Becky walked with their handlers to the row of elevators. Becky gave an eager whine when she heard the soft "ding" of the elevator and stepped inside. She was SO excited for today! Kaia and she had been involved with the renovation of the hospital since the blueprints were drawn. They attended meetings with nurses, doctors, and staff to decide what the new floors should look like and be used for. Although Kaia and Becky mostly snoozed through these meetings, they were delighted to be a part of the process.

The elevator opened, and the dogs stepped into the first floor of the expansion.

"Look who it is. Kaia and Becky!" Two nurses and a doctor walked over to say good morning and pet the dogs.

Kaia felt proud to be part of this special hospital. She had trained for years to learn the important skills needed to help the children staying here. Becky also received the training so that, as a team, they worked together to make the families visiting and staying at the hospital as happy as possible.

New Chapter

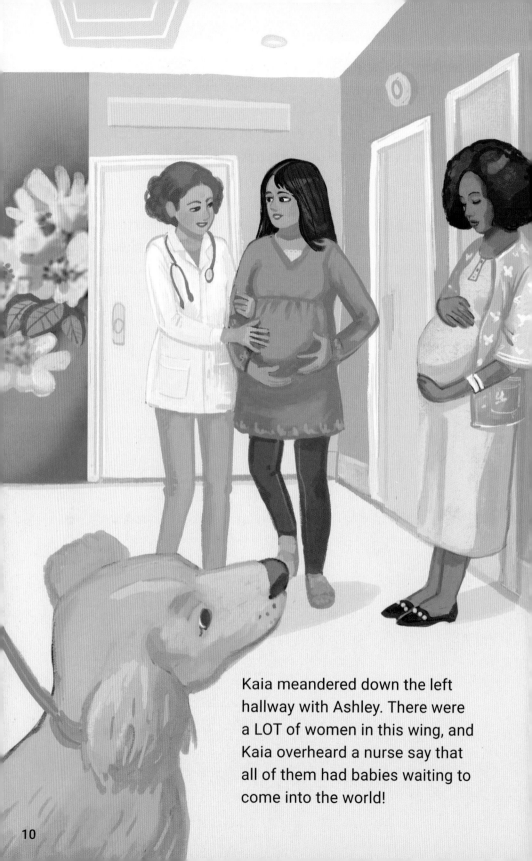

Kaia meandered down the left hallway with Ashley. There were a LOT of women in this wing, and Kaia overheard a nurse say that all of them had babies waiting to come into the world!

Meanwhile, Becky and Erin turned right and headed to the pediatric surgery care unit. Becky liked these new rooms with lots of windows and walls made to look like they opened to the woods, with tree leaves of green and some of red and orange to show the different seasons. There was also paintings of wildlife throughout the new floors.

Becky was ushered into one of the first rooms where an older boy lay in a bed. A nurse stood beside him, checking his chart.

"Becky, this is Jacob." Erin told her. "He's thirteen, and he just had surgery on his back."

Jacob broke into a smile. "Hey Becky. Aren't you a pretty girl?"

"Why don't you take Becky for a walk?" the nurse asked him. "I know your back still hurts, but you can do this. And Becky needs a walk."

Becky waggled her rump and tail for encouragement.

Jacob sighed but reached for Becky's leash as he was helped out of bed. He and Becky walked slowly down the hallway while Erin watched. Becky felt proud, knowing they made a great team.

Passing by the brand new playroom, Becky looked around in wonder. Children were building with blocks and playing with a toy farm. Some were reading or being read to by nurses or their families.

And there was Kaia sitting between a boy and girl about the same age as Jacob. All three kids stared intently as they played a fun football video game on the TV.

"Hey everyone," called Jacob. "I hope to be playing soon, too! "I'm really glad that Becky and Kaia are part of our team," said the girl. Kaia wagged her tail and Becky felt

proud. Everyone cheered when the game-winning play was made. "Touchdown!"

Jacob cheered "WE ARE!"

The others answered the familiar rally: "PENN STATE!"

Jacob walked Becky back to his room. He did a wonderful job walking her, but was tired and needed to rest.

The nurse helped him back to bed. "See you later, Becky," she said. "Jacob will need another walk later today." Jacob groaned, but winked at Becky as she left the room.

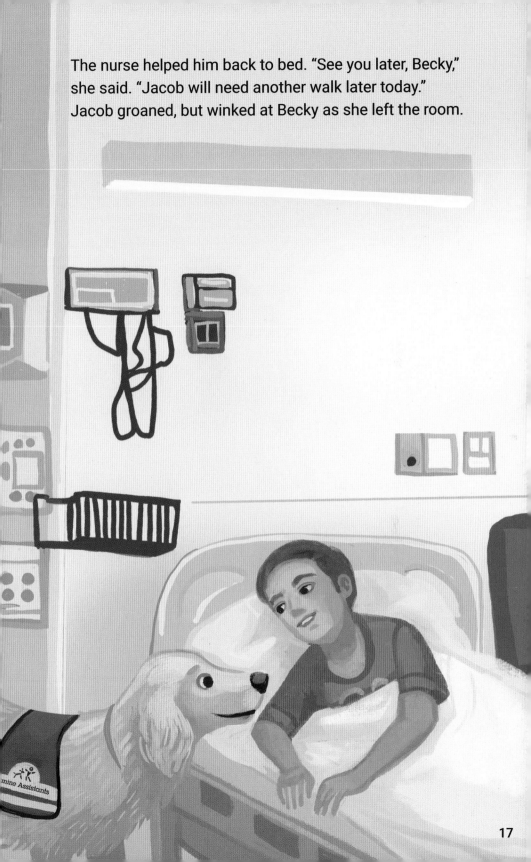

"Great job. Now time for a break!" Erin said. Erin wrestled gently with Becky until she flopped over on the floor so Erin could rub her belly – her favorite job perk!

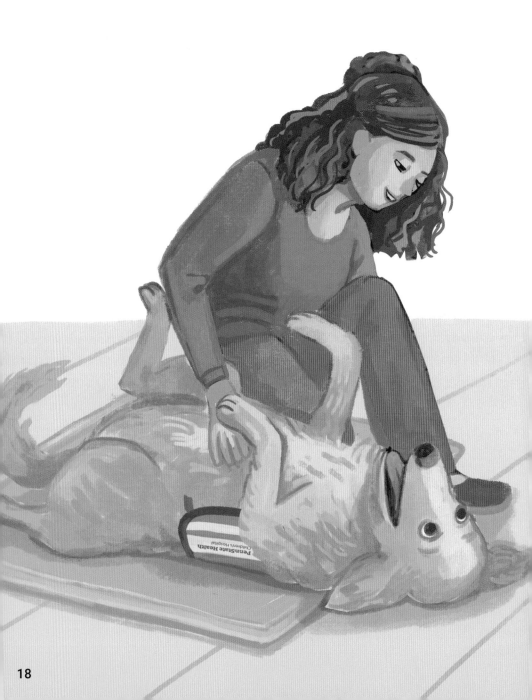

Becky joined Kaia in the playroom and moved over to sit beside a boy working on a craft. He was concentrating so hard, he was sticking his tongue out! Becky nudged his arm and showed the boy her own tongue, flopped down from her lopsided grin.

He giggled. "Hey Becky. Look, I'm making a balloon for Stella's birthday! A bunch of us are. You put these little beads on here and then one of the child life team members melts them together!" Becky raised her eyebrows – how fun!

"Becky!!!" A little girl in a wheelchair joined the group and Becky quickly moved next to her.

"Hi Stella!" The group around the table showed her the balloon crafts. "These are all going to be for your birthday!" The excited kids held up their crafts carefully.

"Just like the balloon that helped Stella get here," said Stella's nurse.

Children's Miracle Network Hospitals

Kaia was a little confused. Did Stella come to the hospital in a hot air balloon? The nurse must have understood the confused look on Kaia's face.

22

"Kaia, this hospital is part of Children's Miracle Network, and people give what they can so families like Stella's are able to receive the help they need. So Stella didn't actually come here in a balloon, but the balloon represents those kind supporters who made Stella's treatment possible. Like the art therapy class where you helped her.

Kaia was impressed. When the kids turned back to their projects, Erin and a nurse moved quickly to Becky, while Kaia walked over to two little girls at a table.

"Kaia wants some tea!" they squealed. They poured her some pretend tea. They also laid out plastic cookies. "Kaia, you can't eat these," one of the girls whispered.

Becky smiled goodbye at Stella as Erin and the nurse walked her briskly down the hall.

"Think she could help with Grace?" Becky overheard the nurse ask.

"Of course." Erin replied.

Erin led Becky into a room with birds painted on the walls. A small girl sat on the bed, looking upset.

"Hi Gracie," the nurse said. "Becky's here to show you how to take your medicine, okay?"

Becky gently put her head on the girl's knee while Erin filled a plastic syringe with some juice.

When it was filled, Becky opened her mouth wide, letting Erin squirt the juice into her mouth. She gave a little lip smack when she was finished. Then she placed her head firmly back on Gracie's knee. Now it was her turn.

Mimicking Becky, Gracie opened her mouth and let the nurse squirt in the medicine. Gracie gulped it down and beamed at Becky, who gave a wink, letting her know she did beautifully.

"Great, job," Erin told her. "Now let's find Kaia for music therapy!"

Kaia was in a room where a music therapist was playing a song on a piano. Some kids sat in chairs with their IVs next to them; some were wheeled in on their wheelchairs. Kaia and Becky walked around the room, accepting all the hugs,

belly rubs, and pets they could get, while the kids sang, played maracas or drums, or just closed their eyes and listened to the melody.

Vahoo-houw bau-ouh!

Suddenly, Becky burst into song herself, adding howling harmonies and making everyone laugh and clap!

After music it was time for lunch and a rest. But first, Kaia wanted to visit the nurses' station. Tugging Ashley in that direction, Kaia gave her best pleading look at a nurse, hoping she would receive a few carrots and some ice to

crunch—one of her favorite snacks! She lucked out. The nurse grinned at her and handed out treats to Kaia and Becky both.

Following Erin and Ashley down the hall, their ice and carrots crunching noisily, they were both now really ready for a nap. Their handlers led them to an office where the dogs found their own special beds to nap on during their busy work day. They both fell asleep right away.

"Kaia, time to wake up!" called Ashley. Kaia yawned. Becky stretched. They had no idea how long they'd slept, but both were rested and ready to get back to work.

"Ladies, we have a very important event to attend" Erin told them as they left their offices. Arriving at their destination, both dogs were overjoyed to see Marcus, a young man with cancer, grinning at them. The hallway was lined with nurses, doctors and patients who clapped and cheered as Marcus stepped forward and rang the bell signaling his

very last chemotherapy treatment. Kaia and Becky knew his was a Four Diamonds family and the way he dealt with his diagnosis and treatment made them so proud to know him and be his four-legged friends! He showed the other patients what the diamonds stood for – courage, wisdom, honesty and strength. Marcus is now in college and learning to be a doctor so that he can help Four Diamonds in their fight to conquer childhood cancer. After all, everything they do is - For The Kids®!

Feeling happy, the dogs headed to the new seventh floor, where moms were tended to after having their babies. It was a calm and peaceful place with lots and lots of babies to view. There were also babies on the eighth floor, including twins and triplets! Walking down the hall, Kaia marveled at how large the new Neonatal Intensive Care Unit rooms were, able to fit all the babies, plus the parents.

Passing by the "neighborhoods," the dogs saw babies who needed extra help and had been grouped together in a room. They overheard a doctor explaining to new parents how seeing other babies helped them all develop!

Kaia meandered over to the Sky Lobby, which was a wide open space where people could look down onto the seventh floor waiting area. She loved how the new floors made the hospital so open and airy. The natural animal theme throughout the floors was also a calming presence.

Kaia noticed a mother sitting in one of the plush chairs. Kaia moved in and the woman's warm smile set Kaia's tail wagging.

"Oh, what a sweet, sweet girl you are!" The woman hugged Kaia and whispered into her ear. "You're just what I needed right now. My sweet baby is recovering. She had surgery on her tiny little heart. I'm so thankful the doctors and nurses could mend her heart. And they helped her breathe on her own, too! Her lungs also needed some special help." Kaia felt tears on her fur.

"These are tears of happiness Kaia, for my baby and for you. I've also missed my pupper who's been waiting for us to come home. Thanks for the snuggle, girl. That helped a lot." The new mom wiped her eyes and smiled. Kaia was happy she could give her a little comfort.

Suddenly, Kaia caught a scent, and eyed Becky to see that she'd smelled it too. They followed their noses into the Ronald McDonald House area, where families could eat together. Someone was making a grilled cheese – yum!

"Okay you two, time to really get back to work," Ashley gently scolded, but there was a smile on her face. While Becky went to help Jacob take another walk, Kaia was taken to a girl named Ellie. She needed to learn to lie very still on a machine that would take special pictures. Kaia jumped up on the exam table and laid down. She didn't move a muscle.

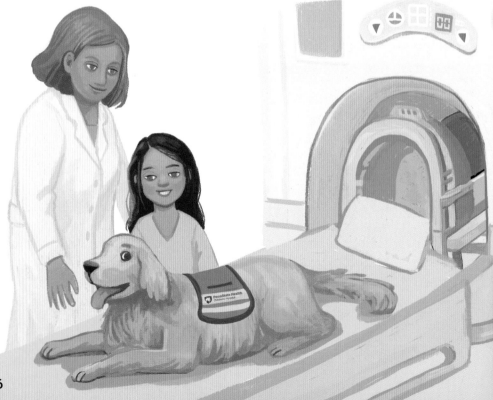

"Good job, Kaia!" praised the technologist working the machine. "Ellie, do you think you can do just what Kaia did and be super still, like you're frozen?" Ellie nodded and climbed onto the table. Kaia was ushered out as the pictures were taken, but went back when Ellie was finished to let her know how great she did.

"Thanks Kaia," Ellie blew out a relieved breath.

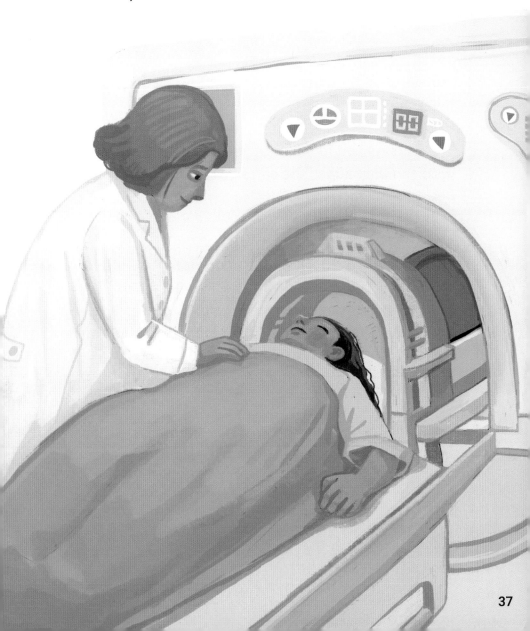

The rest of the day was filled with more appointments, snacks, pets, and belly rubs. At the end of the day, Becky and Kaia met up at the elevators with Erin and Ashley. All four of them were tired and ready to head home.

Before they could leave the lobby though, Kaia and Becky picked up a new scent, one that made them very excited.

"Wow, you're here!" exclaimed Ashley. The dogs turned to see a new handler walking toward them, with a new dog!

"Kaia and Becky, meet your new partner on the Child Life team.

The dogs rushed forward to greet their new friend and partner. Kaia nudged the dog's golden fur with her nose. Becky even dropped her stuffed toy so they could all play with it.

What a day! The hospital expansion was wonderful, and so was this surprise. Kaia and Becky were looking forward to working in their new spaces—helping, comforting, and healing even more patients in the years to come—and now they had a new friend to work with too!

The End

LOVES
belly rubs
her soft toys
singing
grilled cheese
kids
Erin

BECKY

KAIA

LOVES
big hugs
tennis balls
carrots and ice
kids
Ashley

LOVES
cuddling
squeaky toys
bringing back sticks
yummy dog treats
swimming
being around people

NEW ADDITION

Lindsay C. Barry developed her love of reading and writing at a young age, and even more so when she stumbled upon a magical world called Narnia. She is a graduate of Pennsylvania State University and has worked in advertising and executive search.

But her first love has always been writing and education. Her mother, an English, drama, and creative writing teacher, made sure that Barry's love for the literary world was deeply ingrained from a young age.

Barry lives in the Washington, D.C. area with her husband, two sons, two cats, one Bearded Dragon and one Boxer dog. Her sons inspire her life and writing every single day.

Find Lindsay on lbarrybooks.com
Twitter and Instagram @lbarrybooks

Susan Szecsi (say-chee) is an award-winning illustrator and designer. Susan has been drawing since she was able to hold a pencil. She received her classical art training at two prestigious studios in Hungary, the country of her birth. Before becoming a full-time illustrator, she taught art and English, and participated in several exhibitions.

Susan has lived on four continents; she enjoys learning about different cultures. In her free time, she enjoys reading and crafting her own stories. Susan has two sons, and she loves to take long hikes with her husband in the beautiful San Francisco Bay Area, in California, where she lives now.

Find Susan on brainmonsters.com
Twitter @brainmonsters
Instagram @susan_szecsi